GOD WILL NOT FORGIVE

January 2017

Dimitri Kraszennikow

Platinum Creation

God Will Not Forgive

And afterward, I will pour out my Spirit on all people.
Your sons and daughters will prophesize.
Your old men will dream dreams.
Your young men will see visions.
Even on my servants, both men and women,
I will pour out my Spirit in those days
(Joel 2:28-29).

Those of you who betray God's name, will be thrown into the bloody fire

Those of you who will go against Him, will be marked with Satan's stigma

Those of you who will praise the Antichrist, and will take his sign, will suffer eternal torture

If you will take the sign of the beast

God Will Never Forgive You!

(Slawik, 1987)

1. Life before and after

Me

12.07.1987

My name is Wiaczeslaw Kraszennikow (Slawik) born in Russia in 1982, and the first time I visited hell I noticed it looked like a gigantic canyon. It was so steep that no one could climb above it. Its side walls were packed with massive sharp rocks that stuck out like needles. I saw fire, but not the one that you hear about from grandparents who tell you fables at night time. I saw something none of you can even imagine. This fire was aching, pervasive, destructive. It was falling from the sky. It actually looked like the sky was on fire, red, bloody clouds, no sun, and heavy, suffocating smoke floating way above the ground's surface. The stench surrounding the place was unbearable. It was the smell of sulphur, acidic, rotten eggs. It was so heavy and concentrated that it was visibly green. I was able to float around looking for someone who wanted to talk. Many souls were angry, they cursed at me seeing I was able to get out of there. They were so jealous they tried to grab me and force me to stay there. I saw demons, disgusting, greasy creatures cowered in pitch. These demons were there to punish the outcast human souls. They were there to lash them, beat them, stab them with whatever they had in their hands. I saw people stuck in the cauldrons filled with blazing lava. Some of them had only their ankles dipped in it, some were half cowered, but many of them were actually drowning in the lava without getting drowned. Hell is an endless torture, and an endless reminder of their sinful life. Demons constantly follow people on Earth. These evil spirits are continually close to them, whispering into their ears, influencing their decisions, often possessing those of a weak faith. They wait for people to swear, or to steal, or even to kill, then they laugh, and take pleasure from their failure. They wait, and pressure people to sin because they know most of them will eventually do it. Demons stick by their side as they know sooner or later; they will see each other face-to-face. Every single demon says: we have to tempt people; we have to tempt everyone and everywhere no matter who that is. We have to follow all of you because even though some will escape from the evil snare, many will never be able to leave it.

The people's minds are shut for knowledge, not recognising what is real and right. Many of you will not believe in anything I say here, you will laugh and mock my words, you will even mock me. For now. Your minds are fixed and limited. Not true? What would you think when I tell you that I remember my life before I was born? What would you say when I tell you that I was created 150,000 years ago?

Our Father gave me the name Archangel Jeremiel and assigned me with something important. He sent me to Earth in a human body to help people make changes. Just before I was born, I remember walking through a dark tunnel, at the end of which a man in a monk—like robe was standing. He was of an enormous height, similar to twenty feet building. I could feel his eyes on me the whole time. He then pointed out at something. His gigantic fingers were holding a bright reflective lantern, that was hanging down lighting some parts of the place. I slowly got closer to where he was pointing at. And I saw a chasm; one so deep and dark that I couldn't see its end. Then, he pointed out to the other side of the chasm, and at this time, and only for a few seconds, I was able to see what was under this man's robe. A small piece of his livery slid gently to the left side of his breast, slightly uncovering it. What I saw was something blinding, hot and powerful; a light, one that was so bright and dazzling that it prevented me from looking directly at it. I knew who he was. He pointed at the chasm once again before he crossed over it. Thanks to his colossal size he was able to cross over with just one step. The orange reflection from his lantern disappeared soon after, leaving me in limbo, all alone and defenceless. I knew what I had to do. I had to do the same. What if I wasn't able to jump far enough to get to the other side, I asked myself continuously. I had a look at the abyss again but couldn't see its bottom. My body doubled over crushing my unstable legs. I lost my balance and all the confidence I used to have. When everything was lost, I saw Him again on the other side of the chasm raising the lantern above his head. I got up and jumped. Somehow, I hooked to the other side of the chasm, far enough to be able to climb up it. At the very moment when my foot touched the ground, I found myself as a new-born in a hospital next to my mother. I am not allowed to say exactly what kind of world is waiting for some of you up there, as it would influence making one's decisions and choices. Free will is the most important part of the human creation offered by God.

Ever since I was sent to Earth as a human new-born, my mission has been to go against malicious spirits, to heal all kinds of physical and psychological illnesses, but more importantly to warn people of what's coming. Although many people don't listen just now, they don't believe, are ignorant, mendacious and sinful. Some of them may still be swayed when all those things I will mention here later on will happen. At first many of you will adore and cherish me due to the miracle cures you will witness, and all the incisive prophecies I will announce. You will be frightened seeing how I diagnose many of you by scanning your whole body and soul using only my eyes. You will be traumatised to see me talking to something you cannot see or understand, something that you can only feel. You will be impressed with everything you will see and hear. Later when you will notice that the things, I wrote happen one after another, you will begin to resent and hate me. You will follow my book and treat it as a checklist waiting in distress for what's about to happen. You will curse my name as if all of it was my fault and my work. You will demonise me and you Will Be Wrong.

Mama

13.07.1987

My name Walentyna Kraszennikowa, I born in Moscow on 1954. I am Slawik's mama. Exactly one year before Slawik was born my husband take me to Medjugorje. We try for baby for over four years. I pray for miracle, I use all type of herbs to stimulate my organs, but nothing work. My husband speak that we should go to Medjugorje, pray for child. This is place where, as witnessed, Virgin Mary come down from heaven to give her proclamations to chosen ones: Mirjana, Ivanka, Vicka, Ivan, Marija and Jakov. We decide buy travel tickets straight away. When we get there, we see whole village cower in snow. Fields, streets, houses was motionless. There was no clear shapes outside, apart from enormous icicles dangling from rooves, and no colours around apart from white. Hill, also was call Hill of The Virgin Mary, where apparitions take place, was snowless. Smell of grass, flowers especially roses and lilies was overwhelming, but most of all enthralling. As we got closer, we finally start notice pilgrim. They all was guide by priests and other clergy to top. Way there was quite difficult, it was steep, stony, and uneven. Fog float above ground making it difficult to see what was underneath. Differences in temperatures vast, from minus twenty to plus fifteen within few mile zone. We see scientist in different places of hill, sent from Vatican to examine whole area with various equipment. They was trying prove that all these anomalies was cause by location of region and not something supernatural. Medjugorje combine three different time zone, is surround by three dormant volcanos, and gravity is much stronger there than anywhere else. These scientists was investigating this area since the Virgin Mary apparitions begin and was not able explaining anything.

On top of hill was little chapel with white sculpture of Virgin Mary inside. Around chapel we see six young people standing in half circle. These was six visionaries of Virgin Mary apparitions, Mirjana, Ivanka, Vicka, Ivan, Marija and Jakov. They was in hypnotise state, half conscious and unaware of what was surrounding them. I speak to priest Vasily who stand next to me what was happening, and he speak that this is how they look during apparition. They was motionless, staring high at one point. Every now and then, they lift their hands trying to touch or actually touching something or someone. Not long after, Vicka turn around and speak: *'Many of you come today holding evil inside. The White Lady caution that people will be lost if they not change. Redemption will be only possible if you open minds and eyes to see what the reality is. Rosaries are the only way to save humanity.'* All visionaries speak same thing; that people currently live in final times, and whatever will happen, will happen during visionaries lives. White Lady give them all nine secrets about future. They also was assign with personal priest, father confessor Vitko, to who they speak all secrets. All them speak to us, that before worst occur they will be warn ten days before it happens. Seven days before, they start fast, and three days before, father Vitko announce information to world, and spread news across media. People will have only three days to prepare them self.

After we finish prayers, Vicka kneel down. I not sure what happen until people start scream and point fingers to sky. My husband grab me. I look at him and see him cry. I raise up my head and see sun. It was gigantic. It was position only about hundred meters above us. We can feel its heat but no one get burn. It was so bright that we cover eyes with hands. Sun stand still for five minutes and then start spinning around hill in slow motion. Ten minutes after, sun release blast of light similar to nuclear explosion and spread across whole village in few seconds. This blast not cause any damage and only thing it left behind was opposite direction of grass around hill. After that, sun come back to normal position leaving everyone quiet.

After that my husband grab my hand, turn round and walk away with me. Some pilgrim and priests walk with us downhill. About half way down we notice somebody lay on ground. When we get closer, we notice it was woman about forty years of age. Priest who left hill with us start shouting that those next to her, must move away. Priest stop pilgrim and ask everyone to keep praying out loud. Louder they got, more agitate and angry she was. Priest speak that something evil was inside her, something that was damaging her for past ten or even twenty years. Viktor speak that evil hates prayers, church songs, holy pictures, and everything that is remotely connect to church. He also speak that when in range of this things, those who are possessed become aggressive, and violent, and it is often blamed on depression, alcohol and drugs without checking it further.

Viktor kneel down bowing above her head. Under his cassock was heavyweight silver crucifix attach to black leather strap going around his neck. With shaking hand, priest take off his crucifix, and place it firstly on lady forehead, and then on her chest. Priest open his bag and reach for two little plastic bottles in shape of Virgin Mary. One contain holy water, and second one something that look like holy oil. He was preparing himself for exorcisms.

While kneeling next to woman, priest begin by asking:

-*Who are you?* She look at him without blinking, so priest speak again:

-*Who are you?!* Hearing it she squirm from side to side, but said nothing. Priest place his hands on her head and with raise voice speak again:

-*In the name of the Father.* At this point her sweaty limbs assailed towards priest trying to hit him. Someone from our group come closer and hold her legs. Seeing reaction in her priest speak once again -*In the name of the Father.*

She open her mouth and speak -*Fuck you!*

Priest speak again -*In the name of the Father, the Son and the Holy Spirit.*

Woman raise her head and with wide open eyes speak to him -*Fuck you, fuck you, fuck you!*

Priest whisper something for few seconds and speak again -*Depart from this woman!*

She start laugh and with rollicking voice speak -*No, I not want to.*

Priest speak again -*Who are you?*

Woman speak laughing -*Liber* (Latin: free).

Priest -*Oh, so you speak Latin?*

Woman -*Ridiculam vidisti tu sacerdōs stulte* (Funny you notice you stupid priest).

Priest -*Quid vis de muliere* (What you want from this woman?).

Woman -*Nihil de ea, hanc volo!* (I want nothing from her, I want her!).

Priest -*Suntne daemones vobiscum?* (Are there other demons with you?).

Woman -*Sic* (Yes).

Priest -*Quam multi?* (How many?).

Woman -*Tres alii daemones* (Three other demons).

Priest -*In nomine Patris et Spiritus Mariae nomina rewelare ego hodie praecipio vobis!* (In the name of the Holy Father and the Virgin Mary I now command you all to reveal your names!).

Woman -*Libero, Judasz, Hitler, Wasilij Michajłowicz Błochin. Numquid aliud vis nosse retardari ovium irrumator praetor* (Free,

Judas, Hitler, Wasilij Michajłowicz Błochin. Is there anything else you wish to know you retarded sheep fucker?).

Priest -*Non* (No).

Priest -*Sancte Michael Archangele, defende nos in proelio. Contra nequitiam et insidias diaboli esto praesidium. Imperet illi Deus, supplices deprecamur: tuque, Princeps militiae coelestis, Satanam aliosque spiritus malignos, qui ad perditionem animarum pervagantur in mundo, divina virtute, in infernum detrude. Amen.*

(Saint Michael Archangel, defend us in battle. Be our protection against the wickedness and snares of the devil. May God rebuke him, we humbly pray; and do Thou, O Prince of Heavenly Host — by Divine Power of God — cast into hell Satan and all evil spirits who roam throughout world seeking ruin of souls. Amen.)

When he speak amen her body lift up to air, about one meter above ground. It float peacefully in this position for few seconds until priest shout: *'In the name of the Father, the Son, and the Holy Spirit I command you to leave this woman now!'* After third time repeating script, woman body lift up to air even higher, but this time she hover in standing position with her legs and arms twist, and push to sides with huge force. This woman look like crucified Christ on Golgotha hill. There was no howling, screeching, or wailing coming out of her mouth anymore. Agonizing silence fill whole mountain. We smell burning and something that reek as if it was dead for weeks. Horrific smells surround us, stench of sewage, sulphur, virtually sour odours reach our throats through already weakened nostrils, burning our insides. People vomit. Some of them close their eyes. They look like they see but not believe what they witness. I and my husband kneel down as others, and we all pray. We was then singing some songs until priest speak to us to stop. Woman slowly was lower down on ground by something we not see. Her skin change from pale to colour that was not normal yet. Her eyes, especially pupils, was still dark brown. They not go back to previous colour, but according to priest, for her to be normal again, more time, and work was need. Priest speak to her again.

-*What is your name?*

Woman speak -*Stefania Salvago*.

Priest speak to her to go home, rest, and come back next day to church. She was quiet, her body shake, she open her mouth, but say nothing, and leave.

Priest was find dead next day. One of parish nuns was find him in his church in confession room. His body was crush so much that police speak it look like he fall down from at least the tenth floor. His skin was purple from bruises which cover entire body. Every bone in his deform corpse was break and smash into pieces. Few witness speak that woman who priest give exorcisms to, left church in rush same day he died. She throw herself on street, kneel down and shout something in strange language. Some bystanders try to grab and stop her, but her strength was inhuman that prevent them from catch her up. She disappear somewhere in woods. There was also something else. Police find note left by her. It was write in her blood on mirror in one of parish bathroom. It said: '*You Stupid Preachers! Cannot Do Anything Right. Next Time Make Sure You Know How To Do Something Before You Do It. Fuck You -HA-HA-HA.'*

I remember Slawik speak that exorcism are very dangerous. That when priests do them, they must be sure that whatever destruct person from inside, is really gone. Slawik was always very serious when he mention exorcisms. He often warn his visitors that even small contact with occultism, satanic rituals, or something as stupid as ghost calling open gates to hell. Dead priest was not train enough to recognise there was something evil left in that woman.

We decide go back home next day. Heavy snow make our travel twice as long. White, icy fields, gentle fog float above ground, and snow powder cover absolutely everything. No animals, no people outside homes, temperatures reaching minus thirty, it all create mystic and mysterious scenery. Few weeks after we got home, I find out I was pregnant. I remember that when Slawik was two, he speak to me that because we pray on Medjugorje Hill for somebody else instead of us, God decide to give us child. Slawik speak to me: *'I could hear you praying, and I knew you will be the one to be my earthly mother.'*

Slawik also speak to me that since we was back from our trip, I had not one, but fifteen guardian angels watch after me. He speak that guardian angels usually are invisible to human eye, but sometimes they take on human shapes either in people dreams to warn them of coming danger, or they show them self to those who will soon die.

Pregnancy

03.09.1987

About one month before Slawik born, strange things happen. Every night my husband and me wake up at four in morning hearing most terrifying and at same time, most hypnotising music I ever hear. This angelic melody reach us from above ceiling, but every time one of us went upstairs to check what it was, music faded. Tunes of this music change from high to low and then middle ones, synchronise to perfection. These was not some squeaky or high-pitched tunes. These was heart-warming and calming music that almost raise us from our mattress. While tunes was there we was in some sort dream, floating in air.

We was not sure what was this tune or what it mean, but I needed know. In our building in one of houses in bottom floor, hundred years of age old blind babushka rents two rooms. She is known to our all neighbours as well as to all neighbours in different cities located many miles away, as 'the blind omniscient,' 'the lady of hundred virtues,' and 'the hidden eye.' She not have healing powers but can speak with spirits and is contact by them. Good spirits visit babushka to warn about danger. Evil spirits also contact her. But they want her not help others.

I know babushka about ten years, and since I remember, I come into her house to help with chores, and wash her. She not do bad on her own, but like we all do, she need some help. Few year back, at one of my visit in her house, she speak: 'They want me dead, they surrounding me, they suffocating me.' Her skin was white as chalk, without life, as if everything in her body not work. She speak: 'I see them all, they evil, demonic, cover in ash. The smell of putrid meat come of their mouths every time when they shout something. When they swearing, blaspheme against our Lord, and when they assaulting me, stench of rottenness permeates my nostrils, brimming my insides with caustic barf. I see them right now next to you! They laughing so loud, tauntingly. They staring at you, they staring at your belly.' In whole room, the foggy, almost icy air float above floor cause all windows steam. What I witness was something not belong to this world. It feel sad and angry. So powerful and overwhelming try supress my mind and body. One minute I cry and next I want kill. I feel not myself, I feel evil. I must get out of there. Babushka follow me outside her flat. I see in her cloudy-looking eyes that she is troubled. She speak: 'They said they will be back. And that you will be able to see them too, first in your dreams, and then in reality.' Next day new neighbours move in. They look foreign, brownish skin, brownish eyes, maybe from Fareast? It is two of them. I grab my husband to say hello. They have foreign voices but Russian names, his is Borya. He is tall, I can see his ribs and count every bone in his foreign body. Her is Klava. Not see much as weird face cloth hang down her pointy nose. She Not speak much to us, not speak even to each other they both rush with boxes from car to home. My husband look at me, turn around and point his finger on our home. He not want to bother them so we speak we must go. After that we not see them for some time. They is very silent, no noise, no visitors, great neighbours.

Few months later I get terrible dreams. I wake up at four in morning with cramps and shivers. I slowly open my eyes and see this dark shadow beings floating above me. Their cold bodiless forms so close to my face try take over my head. They whisper that dark side is only side I will be safe on. Their voices resonating, coming back to me repeating them self like in echo room, coming and disappearing. I start get vision dreams. I see me cover in blood, laying on floor next to my baby. He cry for hours and get silent. I get same dream every night and, every time at four in morning when wake up, I find myself in room that is as cold and dark as place in my visions. All windows in my house is as steamed as in babushka house. Radiators not work, and all flowers dried out. Something suck life out of myself and everything that is in house with me. Grass outside my building turn brown. All trees is infect with some illness cause them to die. Front of my building look like entrance to old cemetery that was discover three years back fifty miles away. Sometimes I see Klava behind her kitchen window look on my house like she wait for something. Everything die around me. Dead flowers, dead insects, I thought-am I next? I couldn't breathe, I couldn't catch breath. My lungs not work, they was like blocked. My husband speak something to me, I couldn't hear him. I couldn't hear anything. I was breathing, but I was not, I only see dark shapes. Will I stay like that? I will die? My heart race. I could feel its pounding in neck, and in veins. Everything dead around me, and my body shut down. My legs is numb, pins and needles in hands. They was numb. I couldn't see anything. My eyes hurting. They fill with tear. My mouth wide open. I try catch breath, but I couldn't. My mouth fill with tears. I couldn't do it. I couldn't calm down. My heart out of control, leave me on floor motionless. My husband rush me to hospital. Doctors speak it is panic attack, and I am pregnant two month. What that mean, what we do now? My husband drive us back home and park on driveway where babushka stand. With her cloudy, teary, and wide-open eyes, she kneel down, touch my belly and whisper 'blessed human will be born soon.'

Five month later I get to hospital in pain, with blood dripping down from my crutch. After doctors use every tool to help us, they speak they must operate. Baby is born without complications. Me, on other hand, bleed and after operation get to ICU, where I spend whole week connect to hospital wires. Seven days later I move to maternity ward where I see Klava holding her new-born son. I not see her often so not know she is expecting. She look at me and speak-this is little Sasha. Klava body stink from sweat, and baby still cover in dirt make me think they are about to be sorted. So I decide not speak to her and wait for my child. Hour later woman in snow-white uniform, between 16-17 years old, come with my son. She speak: 'your baby was born cover in moles,' and she leave say nothing else. Many times I ask who and where she is but nobody know. After this, when undress my child to bath or change him I check his skin for moles, but not find them.

When Slawik was three months moles cover his whole skin. Both I and my husband take him to local hospital for check-ups. Our paediatrician get urgent call and leave hospital just minutes before we come so other specialist decide to see us. When she examine Slawik, she don't comment his skin but speak: 'This child was born with delicate, almost fragile nervous and psychological system. Please not vaccinate this child. Ever.' She look so sure of her opinion that we don't ask anything else, but after we leave I change mind and decide come back. I walk in and lady doctor is gone. Just like woman in hospital when Slawik is born no one know who she is. She leave note in his files 'Slawik not to be vaccinate.' Although not one doctor know who is that person that write this, apart from one vaccine he get after his birth, Slawik is not vaccinate again. This abnormal existence make me feel trapped and alone but I try make good life for my boy. To feel better next day I take Slawik to park. In the corner I see Klava sit on bench with Sasha on her knees. It is long time since I feel relax but Sasha with his huge eyes, silky skin, and tens of freckles on his cheeks always make me laugh. I come closer to speak to her, and also ask about that face cloth she wear but nearer I get more Slawik is disturb. He punch me, scream, vomit and gasp for air. I think he is tired so I sing him songs but when he turn blue I rush to hospital. I Hear Klava speak something when I leave but not get what. In hospital doctor speak it is normal in child be hysterical with no reason, but after that I promise myself keep him home as often as possible. My living is boring, everything change. I thought Klava will stay away from us but no.

When Slawik and Sasha is about five week Klava start visit us almost every day. I finally ask her about that cloth she wear but she not comment, maybe she has problem with her breath or something. Our boys learn, and observe each other like brothers. As child Slawik develop very quick. He try stand up when he is six months, he speak single words when he turn one, and speak using full sentences seven months after. Sasha try to follow but is bit slow. Sometime if he not do things like Slawik he cry and throws himself on ground like a few year old. Slawik communicate like grownup as soon as he turn two. I remember how little Slawik like sing, but one song is particularly interesting. He often speak how old he really is, and that he need his human body to reach into people head. He use to play next to me and sing this song:

Ах, мама, маменька,	*My mother, my mummy*
Я уж не маленький!	*I am not little anymore!*
Ах, мама, маменька	*My mother, my mummy*
Мне много лет...	*I am really old...*

As short as this song is, it is his favourite. Slawik sing it to me when we cuddle, when he play and I am close. Every time when he speak this amazing story of his creation, he always add these lyrics at the end of it:

My mother, my mummy

I am not little anymore!

My mother, my mummy

I am really old...

2. God, Demons and Angels

The smoke of Satan has entered everywhere. Everywhere! Perhaps we were excluded from the audience with the Pope because they were afraid that such a large number of exorcists might succeed in chasing out the legions of demons that have installed themselves in the Vatican

(Amorth, 2008).

19.12.1987

Walentyna: There is something baffling, and weird going on with Slawik. His huge, brown eyes follow those who come see him. From what I notice, his eyes work like holy water, and x-ray machine. Babushka speak that Slawik sight and eyes is shrewd, instantly penetrate body and mind. Although babushka is blind, Slawik make her sweat. Also those who come see Slawik after his birth, when experience his gaze, left our home and not speak anything. His look is so intense and sharp, that those he stare at know they is scanned. As babushka speak, people is drag into dark side of evil, they not challenge it, and reconcile with whatever is thrown on them. Evil overpowers their bodies and minds, while deriding and mocking their emptiness and limited brain.

There is something so powerful and demanding in Slawik appearance that atheists and those against religion who see him purely to satisfy their own curiosity, change their belief, is baptise and follow Christianity. When Slawik look at people, changes happen. Some start practice religion, or those who not can be save become mentally ill. Unable to overcome their befuddled mind, they kill them self. It is like Slawik gaze, when eye-connecting with evil, activate its dormant, demonic side. These people is find in deserted places away from families. When examine by coroner, each of them have enormous, bloody cuts on chest that is shape into cross inside bloody circle. Cross is turn upside down creating illusion of hanging, bleeding cross. All symbols is cut with serrated blade that left contours ragged. In every case, dead cattle is find close to their bodies, formulating circle around them. These animals is also examine, but cause of death always unknown. Also, blade that is use to make these marks is not find. Their relatives often inform police that before these people is find dead they scream and shout words like: 'haashaala taaku haashala naaduru, ekdebene matena pohaabutu, haashaala naaduru, haashala matena, emane.' They throw them self on ground, can climb walls, cry, and groan at same time. No one is able to stop them, they is uncontrollable, almost completely disconnect from reality.

You must never speak the devil's language idly!

Let this language not become easy in your mouth

or soon it will no longer be your mouth but his.

(Logan,2014)

20.12.1987

Slawik: Even back then I was able, and still am able, to descend my soul to hell. I go there to talk to those who are being punished there for everything bad they did in their lives. When Sasha comes, we often discuss how my abilities can help others, but he doesn't understand. We usually end up arguing, then my mother comes and tell him to leave. Yesterday Sasha came. I was excited to tell him everything about the hell. I asked him to sit down and listen. I told him that I go there to find out how they lived and what exactly they did to deserve being in hell. Many people answer all my questions straight away, even without asking they want to tell me what happened to them. I saw murderers, rapists, alcoholics, all sorts of people who when still alive didn't care enough to change. Everyone can change. Even those who kill can be saved, but only if they change when still alive. People waste their time on earthly pleasures and comforts, ignoring the fact that the life on Earth is something temporary and really short. The life on Earth is in a way the passage to something much more important and permanent, therefore, the way people live on Earth is the only way to establish whether or not they are appropriate for heaven. Sasha listen quietly, and after I finished he stood up and said: 'Your mother brain washed you. Your racist mother lie for fame and money. I know you think everything you see is real but it is not.' My jaw dropped, and cheeks sunk downwards. No words came out of my mouth. I closed my eyes and repeatedly swallowed. I could hear him grinding his teeth, and breathing rapidly next to my face. A few seconds later I opened my eyes and Sasha was gone. I could not stop crying. My friend thinks I am a fraud. My mother rushed in hearing my weeping. She tried to convince me that Sasha is jealous and for my own good it is time for us to stop being friends. My health deteriorated again. I developed such a high fever that I was losing consciousness. My mother was blaming Sasha but I felt like I lost my only brother. I asked her if I can see him, but she refused. For the first time I felt unsure of what my mother's intensions really were, especially that Sasha was the one who could make me feel better. Next day morning I heard knocking. It was Sasha. With his huge, red eyes he looked at my mother, and said: *'I am sorry.'* She let him in straight away. Sasha hugged and hold me so tight I couldn't breathe. He laughed so loudly that my mother thought he was in shock. I was so happy then I fell on the ground again. Something makes me ill. But it doesn't matter because Sasha is with me.

02.01.1988

Today, a thirty-year-old woman came knocking to my door looking for me. She had a little girl lying motionless on her arms. Ginger, long, curly hair, pale skin, purple lips, and yellow bruises on her forehead.

Maria told me that her niece, Wiktoria, was hit by a car when walking back from school and left to die. She was kept in hospital for over a month but doctors couldn't wake her up. Since Maria knew my mother she also knew about me and decided to secretly take her niece from hospital. Sasha let them in and brought straight into my bedroom. It was the first time I was about to physically help someone, and the first time Sasha was about to witness me doing so. My every organ has been squeezed like an orange and deprived from nutrition by the weird fever that's been attacking me since I remember. Because of that I was in bed, hot and drowning in my own sweat, when Maria came. Seeing them I stood up and let Maria rest her down on my bed. Wiktoria was like mannequin, stony, pale, almost dead. I began scanning, the top of her head, her brain, neck, her entire body, bones, and organs. My eyes were going slowly from the left side to right, covering inch by inch of her damaged body. Sasha sat next to her, placed his hand on hers and observed everything carefully. I saw little cracks in her skull, blood clots around her liver, and something that doctors missed. Wiktoria had a small piece of bone stuck in her neck. It cut off the blood flow in one of the major vessels connected with her brain. It also damaged nerves in Wiktoria spine living her paralysed. Her brain turned grey and coarse as the bone blocked the oxygen supply drying out her insides. I laid my left hand on her neck and right on her chest. I raised them up a bit, both at the same time, and with magnetic—like force I sheared it off from the vein and attached the bone back to the vertebra. I raised my hands above her head and slowly moved it down her whole body. I saw her disjointed nerves, and how every nerve fibre braid back together. I saw the cuts, and holes in Wiktoria liver and heart. When the car crashed into her, her organs were squashed with such force they split in many places. Her ribcage was filled with blood clots and shredded flesh. As I moved my hands further the clots started to dissolve, became thinner and permeated into her veins. All the loose pieces welded back into organs, individually filling up her razored meat. Wiktoria opened her mouth and screamed. I wasn't sure why she screamed, it sounded almost like agonizing begging for help. I was about to scan her again but her eye lids began to quiver and slowly raising up. She opened her eyes. Maria nestled me really tightly and ejaculated: 'Thank you, thank you, bless you boy.' I grabbed Wiktoria's hands and helped her to sit up. She was very unsteady so I asked Sasha to stand behind her and support her back with his knees. During that time Sasha said nothing, but he also did not move his eyes away from her. I guided Wiktoria with my hands to slowly stand her up and she followed. She stood up holding my hands and moved forward. With the smile on her face she did a few steps, closed her eyes, and collapsed. Seeing this, Sasha grabbed his jumper and ran away. I quickly kneeled down trying to revive her but nothing worked, my prayers, my healing, everything failed. She died in front of me. Maria kneeled down next to me and shook Wiktoria shoulders repeatedly. She tried to wake her up. 'It's too late'- I said, 'she died.'. I felt the acidic burning on my cheeks from the countless slaps Maria punished me with. My mother walked in, grabbed her hair and pushed her out of my room. I heard weeping, screaming, banging and then silence. She walked in again, took Wiktoria's body and left. 'What happened? Why?' I asked my mother, 'Why?' I repeated. She touched my face, kissed my bruised cheeks, and also left saying nothing. What is wrong with me?

Sasha came back the next morning apologising, saying he ran away because he was in shock. I was in bed crying, couldn't understand what happened. Sasha sat next to me and said: 'For your own good it is time to stop, and do it now.' When Sasha left, my mother came again, sat on my bed and said: 'Two angels travel across villages in Poland. They try really hard find place to rest before nightfall. They knock on door of wealthy family. What they find inside is rudeness, swearing, and parsimony. They was tell to go to basement, and rest on floor. They do what they was tell to do. While in basement older angel notice hole in wall which he immediately patched up. Other angel ask: 'Why you help this family if only thing we get from them is night in cold basement on hard concrete floor?' Angel reply: 'Things are not always what they seem.' Next day two angels get back on road, and again try find place to stay before nightfall. This time they knock at poor farmer's house who, unlike first family, welcome them with everything he and his family has. Both he and his wife decide give away their own bed for night to make their guests comfortable. Next morning, when angels wake up, they see farmer and his wife on knees, with bloody, teary eyes, and their faces unable to express anything but sadness. Both in each other's arms, they ask angels why God allow death of only cow they has, from which the farmer's family get fresh milk every day. Younger angel left house crying and shaking his head from one side to other. Other angel rush after him. 'Why?' Younger angel ask. 'Why, did you help first family when they was hostile to us? And why you let their only cow die, when farmer's family show us nothing but love and appreciation?' Older angel reply again: 'Things are not always what they seem.' He continue by saying: 'Man from first house got sly, and hostile to others when he got rich. When we was in basement I notice big hole in wall. When I got close, I see hidden money in wall. Homeowner hid most of money in there to avoid sharing it with anybody else. I decide cover hole so owner will never find it. In second house, in middle of night, I see angel of death who come to take farmer's wife. I give him his cow instead. Things are not always what they seem.'

My mother looked into my eyes and repeated: 'Remember- things are not always what they seem.'

3. Healings, Helping, and Hatred

And He said, Hear now my words. If there is a prophet among you, I Yahweh will make myself known to him in a vision. I will speak with him in a dream

(Numbers 12:6).

04.09.1989

Walentyna: When Slawik turn seven he and Sasha start school that is twenty-minute walk from our farm. His teacher is our neighbour. One day Slawik speak to her that he see baby girl inside her womb. She not believe him, nor anybody else. Her gynaecologist confirm pregnancy week later. Word about his abilities spread across whole school and our village. People was coming day and night ask Slawik to speak their future. Sasha parents disappear last year and since then he stay with us. Slawik is happy as Sasha help him speak to this people. Sasha heart is very good so he let in everybody even when Slawik is very sick, then I must ask them all to leave. Sasha not understand and he speak to Slawik: 'Since you are the one to save us all don't let your weak mother be part of it.' Slawik ask me to stay away and I am. Situation with crowd outside my home become serious and force me to contact Orthodox Church representative in Miass town locate roughly twenty-three kilometres from our village. He is call orthodox pope, father Vladimir Ziemianowa. Sasha come with us. When father Ziemianowa see Slawik, he grab his hand and walk him straight to statue of Virgin Mary. I and Sasha not allow to listen anything they speak, and we get ask to wait outside. About hour later, father Ziemianowa come and speak exact words that babushka speak, that my son is good person. Sasha lips move from side to side and eye lids drop down half way when pope speak to Slawik. His eyes follow Ziemianowa all that time. Pope notice, come closer, whisper something to Sasha ear and leave. Sasha cheeks raise up and eyes open wide. He look happy so not ask him anything. We take train back home same day. People sit tight, squashing each other. Slawik manage sit opposite me. He rest his head on window and his eyes close. Sasha squeezed between and another man. The way is long so I close my eyes too. About ten minutes before we reach our destination someone pull emergency brake. All light is off. People scream, run from one wagon to another. Sasha jump on my knees and next thing I see, Slawik disappear. Guard signal train move, and journey return to normal but Slawik is gone. I raise alarm, but guard speak to me to leave train. He speak that me crazy, and that no child sit opposite me in train. I ran straight to police station. They begin search. They tell me go home. I open door and my husband see me and Sasha, no Slawik. I tell him. He shout and cry at same time, hit wall with fist and kneel down in front of me and speak why I let anybody take him? Why I am so stupid to not notice someone take him? What mother I am? I kneel down next to him try to understand how this happen, but I couldn't. At about six in morning two police officers knock on door. They speak that body of child is find, and that it is boy. They take us to mortuary straight away to identify his body. My husband hold my hand but avoid looking at me. I see drop of sweat on his pale forehead. I know he not want to look, but we have no choice. They uncover its tiny, naked body. He have dark bruises on skin and blood under his nails. Doctors speak that someone rape him, beat, and kill him shortly after. But it not Slawik. It is our neighbour son who missing same day our Slawik. Few days after, knocking to door again. Cup in my hand drop down and my powerless body crumple on floor.

My husband grab my waist and try lift me up, but when he see Slawik open door, his body collapse next to me. Sasha see him, but not move. Static gaze, passive face. Slawik walk in and sit next to him. Sasha start cry, hit Slawik and shout: 'Why did you come back? Why?' I rush and cuddle them both. Sasha already lost his parents. So much pain in this little boy.

05.09.1989

Slawik: The day before our trip to Miass, I had a vision. A man walking towards me with a gun. When I saw him on the train I knew what was about to happen. It had to happen. I could read his mind. He wanted to take me to his house, lock me in one of his rooms, and get drunk. I saw him crying. The next morning after waking up he wanted to shoot me, and bury my body in the nearby woods. I also saw something else. This then religious man lost his child to cancer and rejected God. Soon after demons possessed him. They wait for people to break down. They are always on their guard day and night, ready to attack. This is exactly what I saw when I looked at him in my dreams and then in reality: demons— dark, greasy, deformed beings. When he passed out from the alcohol I managed to unlock the door. I stood above him, and placed my hands on his forehead. I prayed to God to exile these demons back to hell, to leave this man in peace. They were gone as soon as I finished my prayers. When he woke up he said he couldn't hear voices in his head anymore, voices that poisoned him. He was Satan's marionette for nearly a year. He brought me back home to apologise but also to give himself up to the police. This is what he wanted. Redemption.

06.09.1989

Walentyna: Slawik is here to help people, and make them aware of what is coming. He speak persistently: *'I am the last one sent to Earth, and I told people everything there is to know, and no one else will be sent to repeat what was already said, because those who are similar to myself will not be sent by God again.'* One day, when I was alone with Slawik, he speak he can see people interior organs. He speak that he see people illnesses, and he know exactly how they begin. Slawik speak that sick people excrete unpleasant odour from their body. That this smell is like mixture of fungus feet with human sewage. He also speak that sick people always has black shadow around them. In contrast, Slawik speak, that new-born babies is always surround by bright, clean, almost fresh emanating light. This, though, change during their live when they start to eat not organic food, smoke, and fill their bodies with tablets and drugs. Slawik speak that people get spots, infections, diarrhoea, and other symptoms when their organs are about to give up. *'They don't care'*- he speak- *'they just don't care!'*

Slawik speak to me that he can read our president mind, but also mind of president of America. He speak that he know exact place where military stores rockets, and where nuclear weapons is hidden. Slawik speak that he read every person mind and there is just no secrets for him on Earth.

10.09.1989

Walentyna: When Slawik was well enough to go to school, teachers try to pressure him to cut his hair short, but he refuse. He speak: 'I will grow it long just like Christ did.' He suffer abuse from children. They lock him up in toilet, call him animal, they laugh at him every time he walk by. Slawik teachers try force him to cut his hair, they even come to our house to pressure me, but I speak to them I have no influence over his decisions, and no right to speak what he must do. Slawik is not the top student in school, and often come back home upset. He negate teachers sentences, and call their lessons misleading. Many times after school he speak to me that it is painful to listen to all these lies teachers spread, because he knows from God what is truth. When doing his homework he force himself to do it in way teachers want. And when he get high mark, he show it to me and speak: 'For you mummy, to make you feel better.'

11.09.1989

Walentyna: Last Saturday morning, married couple come ask for help. Slawik not hesitate and invite them straight away. For some reason, Slawik speak only with woman, and her husband stand next to her quiet, cupping fist in other hand. He decide walk outside to smoke. Wife speak that someone steal their car, and Slawik must help get it back. Slawik touch her hand, close eyes and speak: 'your car is hidden very close from where we are. Immediately after the level crossing is abandoned house. It has massive gaps between bricks, many cracks caused by floods, and holes in walls just above the ground. At end of back garden is an old barn where your car is hidden under haystack.' Women speak to Slawik, who steal it? Just then her husband walk in, Slawik point finger where he is and speak: 'he did.' He spit on floor, grab wife hand and leave in rush. Woman return next day to thank Slawik for his help and let him know she find her car. I speak to her why her husband steal it. She speak they is in middle of divorce and, under cover of robbery, he want to keep car for him.

When Slawik begin help people, he speak that he must not take single rouble from anyone. Slawik warn that I also must not accept any money from people, just as he must not. I speak: 'when and who speak to you all these thing?' And he speak: 'I am able to hear it since I can remember, and the voice is always one. It's womanly, and soothing. And your voices seem to be dead next to hers. And thanks to her I know the past, the present and the future. Everything was disclosed to me.'

20.09.1989

Slawik: Some people tried to force me to accept their money. They often begged me to take at least half of the amount they offered, but I always refused. They then put them imperceptibly into my pocket when saying goodbye. Some placed money on the kitchen counter, hide them behind larger items, and even tried to hide it inside the bathroom and my bedroom. Every time, when someone left something for me, my testicles squirmed inside causing an instant sickness. I started to sweat, the colour drained from my face and the paleness spread across my whole body. I knew what they did. What seemed to be right for people, was killing me. Seeing my health deteriorating my mother rushed to search the whole house, and gave back the money she found to those who left it behind. I heard many times from her that she saw how people behind my back give money to Sasha who accepts them with a smile on his face. There was something between them two that I couldn't understand. She often accuse him of stealing and lying. He then cries, and comes to me saying she hates him. I trust Sasha, he is like my brother, and slowly I start to think the problems are in my mother's head.

By the time most of the people from my village had already met me, the whole community was in ferment and started to buzz due to what they had seen and experienced with me. Unfortunately, this promulgation brought closer to me those against me and God. Every day I see demons outside my window. They come with people who try to lure me to their side. These are practitioners of energy medicine, Jehovah witnesses, ecumenicists, Baptists, Hare Krishna followers, different kinds of conjurer men and sorcerers, Masons, and Messing followers, and many others that adhere to various cults. Although these demons don't enter my house, they still wait outside. I can tell they are fuming, they hit the windows, shake their heads from side to side, show me obscene hand gestures, spit on the walls and windows. They shout: 'We will burn you off! You will not live! Either you will stop helping others, and stop doing good deeds, you will join us and become an amazing practitioner of energy medicine, you will live in wealth and have absolutely everything, or we will burn you off!' These people who are followed by demons try to persuade me that I am the one that is evil and the only way to save my soul is to change sides and join them.

Sasha always listens to these conversations, and tells me to think about it. He says: 'please, listen to them brother, they are old and wise and know more than you ever will'. Usually I hear them out, but when I try to explain how wrong they are, they leave my house running. Sasha never leaves. Sometimes I think Sasha is able to see demons because when they appear he always stares directly at them. But I know it is impossible. People's perception about evil doesn't even half-cover what hell and demons look like. If people were able to see it all, they wouldn't be able to cope and their hearts would blow up out of fear. This is why God had to close humanity's physical sight on the spirit world for most people, to give them the ability to make decisions without living in constant fear.

My mother used to say that people will soon be living in fear no matter if they are believers or not. The New World Order is about to begin without people realising. Some don't believe her. Some say she made me her 'living marionette.' But did she? Some will say anything to make us look insane, but I know that these people already chose. Everyone has time to believe now, but the time will come when it will be too late for them to change. When the time will come, God will not be merciful anymore.

4. Visions. How to survive during the reign of the Antichrist.

Islam is coming to take over Germany whether you want it or not...not through war but by the fact that Germans don't reproduce and Muslims have 7-8 children each...but not only that, your daughters will marry bearded Muslims and wear the hijab, their sons will wear a beard! The Muslims will have four wives and 27 children and what does the German man have? One child and maybe a little pet dog! The German has taken advantage of the Muslim for too long, just so he can drive his Mercedes... now Islam is coming and your daughters will wear the hijab!

(Spencer, 2015)

04.12.1989

Walentyna: I often ask Slawik why God send him. And his answer is always same 'mummy I came here to save people.' He come here to admonish people because whole world will be lost due to people reckless and egoistic need to live in wealth. Slawik speak not accept anything from Satan, which is weird because how we know what we get from Satan? But Slawik know.

04.01.1990

Slawik: The female voice came to me last night again. The tone of her voice often steady and calm, now low, and trembling. She asked me not to trust anybody, especially those who are close to me. Not everything the lady says is always clear but my mother and Sasha are now the only ones I will trust. She didn't say anything else but she showed me. In my vision I saw what appeared to be a small, very pleasant looking, grey plate. This is the world's passport-she said, that will be created straight after biochips. When people will go to pick it up from local offices, or embassies, a small device will scan their foreheads, or their right hands. At the same time, this device, by the use of some isotopic rays, will tattoo on their foreheads, or on their right hands, three numbers '666' - the sign of the beast. She repeated: Tell them all- those, who will take the sign, *God Will Not Forgive!*

06.01.1990

Slawik: Sasha came to me this morning. I told him what happened last night. He raised his eyebrows and looked at me. He then sat next to me and tried to persuade me that it is not my responsibility to help anybody. I turned my away from him. With raised, shaking voice he stood up and said: 'who do you think you are? If you think you are the chosen one, you really are crazy!' I looked at him but no words came out of my mouth. He slammed the door and left. Am I? Am I crazy? No! I need to beg you, simple people— don't take biochips, don't become zombies at your own wish. Are you able to imagine—Satan's marionette created from the child of God? The hundreds of invisible strands will be attached to every marionette. And all these strands will be in the hands of Satan. Whichever strand he pulls, the marionette will do everything he wants it to do. Can you imagine, you with microchips: Satan pulls one strand and all microchipped cry, he pulls another one and all chipped laugh. Will they still be called people? *Think!* You all have to come to your senses. You are not blind, though many of you have tunnel vision. Why don't you listen to those from different countries? They tell you how it is, they tell you God exists! You need to be afraid of God! There is nothing else I want to say but this: don't take the microchips. Don't apply for the 'world's passport', because those who accept the micro schema, will then be pulled by a string, and ‘willingly’ will go to take the sign of the beast. I don’t understand why so many people go towards the darkness. Why, just for the spoils, they betray God? You have to open your minds now, because, since the microchips are already in use, the sign of the beast will be ready for everyone soon.

06.01.1990

Walentyna: You all, just think... Look at your grandchildren and children. What they could or can speak to you at age of seven or eight? Can they heal you? No, they not. Can they speak to you not to take these microchips, or what God likes and dislikes? No, they not. So listen to this little prophet, who said: ‘don’t take these microchips under your skin, because those who will, will also have to take the sign of the beast!’ If someone was already chipped, must try get rid of it straight away. Perhaps, there still may be something that can be done. More people that will be microchipped, quicker world will become extinct. Why not be faithful to God, why be faithful to antichrist? Why live in coma? Children are kill, children are rape, demons do it all. These not stories, this real. People from different parts of our country come here, and speak same thing over and over again. These not lies. They all see what happen.

10.01.1990

Slawik: Last night I had a dream that the time on Earth will soon come, when only one global ruler will be chosen. The antichrist. He will allow everything that the church prohibited since its creation. He will clarify himself to the whole world by saying that God doesn't need people to be suppressed by rules and morals. He will explain that everything on Earth was created for people to take advantage, and pleasure, out of. The people will be furious. They will be enraged thinking that the Holy Church taught them incorrectly. The people will follow the antichrist's education, which will reassure them that God doesn't need people's abstinence, and fasting, and therefore they will completely abandon the devout life.

11.01.1990

Walentyna: Slawik often hold his hand on his chest, and with shaking voice speak to me: 'mummy I feel pain in my chest, I feel sick. Why are they all so blind? Why they want to be evil? Mummy, if you could see how shameless, and lecherous woman are. The closer Jesus's coming is, the more shameless people become!'

12.01.1990

Walentyna: Last night Slawik wake up screaming again. I rush to his bedroom. He sit in corner, wet and shaky. He speak that in his dream he see that when antichrist show his false miracles to deceive people of his holiness, he will successively pronounce himself as God. Slawik hold his head and cry when tell me this. He weep that most Christian will see in him Christ, Muslim will see Mahomet, and Buddhist, Buddha. And only some Buddhist will not be convince of his holiness, as in their religion, Buddha was not expect to come down to Earth. Slawik speak: 'Why? Why mummy? Why? It hurts; really hurts.'

20.02.1990

Slawik: Yesterday evening, my mother had to go to babushka again. I had fever so she left me in bed. Sasha stayed with me. Not long after I heard knocking on my window. I stood up but could not see anyone. I opened the window to check if anybody was there but shut it back as the frost settled on my eyebrows. I rushed back to bed. Sasha touched my head and said: 'No one knocked. You are burning out. Go back to sleep.' I felt that the temperature in the room dropped down. I grabbed blanket and covered myself up to my eyes. My breathing became rhythmic, but heavy. The stiff chilly air sucked by my nostrils was pushed out from my mouth as the white fog. And I heard voice. Sasha looked at me again, raised his voice and said: 'sleep.' I went under the blanket. And I heard her voice again. The female, soothing voice whispering to my ear that in a few seconds I will see something important. She whispered: 'Don't talk, just watch and listen.' It was him again. I saw tens of demons surrounding the antichrist. I saw that the people from different religions will see their own god in him. All these demons next to him will look like angels, pure and delicate. There will be only a few people who won't believe him, but all the rest will follow him blindly.

I can see him right now, as if he was standing in front of me. He looks straight into my eyes with such hatred, and whispers that those who listen to me will be dead soon. This creature looks evil, and is brazen. With his face so white, and lifeless, it appears virtually paralysed. His skin without any pigmentation looks as if was covered in flour. His bushy ginger eyebrows raised up at all times, cover only a small part of his blemished, scarred face. His left eye looks wide open, however the right one is swollen, and covered in green pus. I can see that the body of the antichrist will be malodorous. The stench of sewage coming out of his body will be unbearable, but no human will notice it. The antichrist will be able to move mountains. He will be able to move the mountains from beyond the sea. And people will touch them to make sure his miracles are real. They will all place their hands on these mountains, and they will feel its texture. But there will be no mountains. They will see whatever the beast wants them to see. But the fire from heaven shown to them all, the fire will be real. The voice disappeared. I uncovered my head and began telling Sasha what I heard; and he laughed, placed hands on his belly and laughed even louder. He then dropped down on floor, lied on his back, and while waving his legs and arms like a spider he shouted laughing: 'your imagination kills me.'

The God Will Not Forgive!

03.03.1990

Walentyna: I remember Slawik speak, that in Soviet time, in some Moscow hospitals, without families know, new-borns was microchipped. Later, parents is puzzled why children is born so smart. I see now that, in today world, everything Slawik speak is true, and that microchips is ready for us. Media are proud to announce in local news and radio that life biochips are prepare as we speak. What exactly is it? Who is owner, who by use of this microelement will take over our mind, and even smallest cell in our organism? Who will we be? Slawik speak that everyone must decide now what they want do as to issue even smallest certificate, people will hear: 'Unless you will take the number (the sign of the beast), we will not be able to give you your certificate.'

And another angel, a third one, followed them, saying with a loud voice, 'If anyone worships the beast and his image, and receives a mark on his forehead or upon his hand, he also will drink of the wine of the wrath of God, which is mixed in full strength in the cup of His anger; and he will be tormented with fire and brimstone in the presence of the holy angels and in the presence of the Lamb.'

(Revelation 14:9)

Everything people must know is already write centuries ago. But you don't read, and don't listen. Just read this:

And he causes all, the small and the great, and the rich and the poor, and the freemen and the slaves, to be given a mark on their right hand or on their forehead, and he provides that no one will be able to buy or to sell, except the one who has the mark, either the name of the beast or the number of his name. Here is wisdom. Let him who has understanding calculate the number of the beast, for the number is that of a man; and his number is Six Hundred And Sixty-Six

(Revelation 13:16).

Slawik speak that in his vision he see that on beginning, these numbers not be visible on microchipped. This change soon after; mark of beast become digital like. It turn to bright, green numbers showing those who is microchipped. If microchipped try remove these numbers by cutting off his hand, these numbers appear on stump. If this person body is then cut into small pieces, then these numbers appear on every single piece of his remains. In beginning, people is ashamed, and try everything to hide this numbers. The longer this mark stay on them, braver these people become and proudly carry sign of antichrist.

So the first angel went and poured out his bowl on the Earth; and it became a loathsome and malignant sore on the people who had the mark of the beast and who worshiped his image

(Revelation 16:2).

15.05.1990

Slawik: I had another vision last night. I saw that those who will not betray God, and will stay faithful to him, the Lord will hide, and protect them with such power that the evil will not be able to defeat them. Those people will live in small settlements, and they will simply be invisible to their enemies. Those, who will not betray God, they will not change at all, they will stay ordinary, and this will be their victory. I saw there will be a settlement into which no one who carries the sign will be able to enter. The whole place will be surrounded by the moat brimming with water. Although this place will be tightly secured, I saw that one person will successfully approach to the exterior wall. This, however, will be stopped by God's power, which will raise the living zombie up in the air and throw him on the other side of the moat. I saw him soaked with anger, but walking away.

For those people, who will take on the sign of the antichrist, the special shops will be created, in which the best commodity and groceries will be available. For those, who will not accept the sign, there will be some shops opened, but the items there will be of poor quality, and much more expensive. Later on, in order to pressure those unmarked ones to accept the sign, these shops will be defunct. I saw that the antichrist will corrupt the young people by allowing them to do anything they want. He will assent all addictions and deviations, and people will follow his law. I see that God will protect these unmarked ones, and although they will suffer, none of them will die from starvation. For a short time only, these people will suffer and God will rush to help them, together with his angels. They will all protect only those who did not betray Him. The time will arrive soon after, when even the marked ones will be forbidden to purchase anything. Only then they will realise they have been tricked, but it will be too late. Their rage will be pointless. They will suffer from innumerable diseases and will be tortured by festering and rotting wounds. Their anger will be turned especially at those who didn't take the beast's numbers. Those unmarked ones will be constantly in danger. The lack of food will force the weaker people to go to the shop for groceries. These people will be checked there for the numbers *666*, and if none are found, the cashiers will forcefully tattoo them on their forehead, or the right hand. Those who willingly, or unknowingly, take the sign won't be able to die. If such a person will try to kill himself by driving into a brick wall, and his body will be ripped apart into pieces, then it will, like a monster from a horror movie, be reconnected back together, and resurrected.

In those days people will seek death, but they won't find it. They will want to die, but death will run away from them

(Revelation 9:6).

I saw that the antichrist will stiltedly create a global famine, which will consume millions of lives. In some places on Earth the children will die from starvation, however Moscow at that time will brazenly wallow. Not for long though. The whole of Moscow will slowly be buried under the ground due to the destructive tectonics movements. And when the Son of God will touch the Red Square with his foot, then the rest of the Kremlin together with its star will be buried as the last ones. When this will happen, the Russian's leader will move to Bonn in Germany, and from there he will rule the residue of his country.

07.08.1990

Slawik: The lady told me last night that the time will come when friends and family will betray each other. The priests, monks, and Christians will be hunted down and killed. She also said that almost every place on Earth will be wiretapped, and even people on the streets will be terrified to speak. These times will be much worse than when Stalin was alive. Many people will turn to Spiritualism, which automatically will open the gates into the ghostly world. Their lives will be controlled by demons. The marked ones will hear demons' voices, and will even be able to speak with them. These people will consider their abilities as the 'greater mind', or the 'seventh sense' not realising they have been manipulated by demons. But God Will Not Desert Those Who Didn't Betray Him.

But the lady said there is hope for those who listened. She whispered:

God will wipe away every tear from their eyes, and death shall be no more, neither shall there be mourning, nor crying, nor pain anymore, for the former things have passed away

(Revelation 21:4).

Walentyna: Slawik is always very upset when speak about future. Sometimes, when I come back from shops, I see him kneel down in corner of his bedroom, asking God in tears to 'save all these poor people.' Later, he come to me and speak that, although he know that future he see must happen so evil can be defeat, he still feels as if he is defeat.

Behold, I am coming quickly, and My reward is with Me, to render to every man according to what he has done

(Revelation 22:12).

The Awakening

20.02.1991

Slawik: The visions occur every night now. Sasha says it is my deteriorating health playing tricks on my brain but is this even possible? I saw again that most of the forgotten diseases will come back. There will be decaying, bloated corpses lying on the streets, and no one will bury them. Some of them will have their eyes wide open as if their bodies went into some weird spasm. The dried, almost black blood will cover their cracked, blue lips. The worms and maggots will crawl out of their nostrils, eyes, ears and mouths. The stench of gasses coming out of their bodies will be worse than the reek coming out of the sewage, the stagnant water, and the rotten meat all together. The people will be dying while walking, and crawling. The human bodies will be weak, and completely deprived of energy, which will severely debilitate their immune system. My town will not be any different. Whatever Will Happen Elsewhere Will Also Occur In Russia.

I saw our building outside of which is an old, rusty bench. I can see a woman that walks towards this building, but notices her female friend on that bench. She is dying. I see that this woman wants to stop and help her friend, but she is too terrified to stop in case she will get too weak to get back home to her children. So she passes by, sobbing, and hitting her chest with the soaked, sweaty fist.

21.03.1991

Walentyna: I remember that once in our kitchen, me and Slawik drink tea. We speak about his school, and I feel sharp, needle like pain inside my eyes. I not see clearly. In fact, only things I see, is big, black dots pulsing and spinning around me. It feel like my head is about to explode. Slawik notice it, and speak to me: 'Mother, the demons constantly attack people overhand. The demonic energy in the formula of the black dust, continually moves with an extreme speed, trying to drive and enter the human body. When demons are not successful, the people still suffer from a sharp pain in various places in their body, just like you mother right now.'

12.05.1991

Slawik: Another night, another vision. In December, 1991, the whole Caucasus will be shaken by one of the bloodiest, never-ending wars. I see small children on the ground, lying down next to relatives. Next to them I see other civilians, old, blind people. Not moving, not breathing. All with gun shots, with missing limbs, covered in their own body parts. I see the total destruction of the Caucasian cities and villages.

Raisa Gorbachev, the wife of the soviet leader Mikhail Gorbachev, in the near future, will have some serious head problems. She will recover, however, shortly after, she will be diagnosed with a rare blood disease that will kill her in Germany. After Raisa's death, Gorbachev will be left alone, and completely superfluous. Russia's internal political problems won't be over. Boris Yeltsin, the Russian president, will also suffer from very serious health problems, however he will not die, but eventually will have to resign. Yeltsin will be succeeded by someone not known at that time. This man, unlike the others, will not belong to any political party. But he will not be the last Russian president. The last president will be the one who reveals the whole truth about Gorbachev, and Yeltsin.

The time will come when the wages and the prices in shops will be increased. This will change about a year and half to two years before the beginning of the worldwide famine, when the government will leave the higher wages, and will cut shops prices. At that time, the work of customs officers will drastically change. They will allow everything into the country. First, the quality of goods getting into Russia will be extremely poor. Later, this will slightly improve. The false illusion will be created, that the quality of life progresses. Then food from the stores will be hidden underground by those in power, and the stilted famine will begin. I see Russia shares its resources with the other countries. Due to the rising hunger, no one will decline any help, not even from Russia.

29.10.1991

Walentyna: Slawik speak to me, that people soon witness various signs on Earth, in sky, even on moon. He warn me not look at them, as they are demonic. People will forget everything that evangel says about them, and bible speak about false happenings and miracles at end of time. These demonic signs will deceive people. Slawik speak to me that there are many demons on moon, and on sun. They will show tricks that will consume curious minds. Slawik speak: 'Mother, you cannot care about any of these signs. As interesting as they will be, you cannot look at them. These will be the signs and the tricks from the beast.'

01.11.1991

Slawik: The whole world, including Russia, will be divided into smaller areas, which will help to maintain the better quality of life. These areas will be helping each other, until the global catastrophes occur. Then, every region will be occupied only with their own welfare. The power blackout will begin from the Far East, and will continue globally. The gas supply will have to be cut off completely due to the earthquakes, and powerful tectonic movements. In some regions, the children will be freezing to death. The cities and villages will drown in darkness and cold. There will be no heating. Not in the schools, or in the nurseries, nowhere. At first, the teachers will put on heavy coats to stay warm, and will continue to educate these remaining pupils. There will be no notebooks left, nor chalk the teachers use to write with on the boards. The children will use the already filled pages to write in their margins. Eventually, the lack of school supplies will force the teachers to close all institutions. The children will roam on the lifeless streets with no purpose, and no hope. Due to the lack of gas and electricity, all of the factories in Chelyabinsk will be shut down. For some reason, only the fire stations will function, but these too will be deserted later on. The most gigantic buildings and constructions will be swallowed by the soil. Also, all of the solitary factories and empty houses will disappear under the ground. The drought will become more and more pervasive. I see how the water is disappearing from the Earth's surface. It looks almost like it's escaping from its sources. All the survivors will be left with nothing. Their bodies, after just a few days, will look like dried branches. I see them holding their own teeth, which most likely fell out due to lack of nutrients. Only those, who prepared themselves for the end of times will know, that if you put a cross next to the well, the water will always be in it. In every other place on Earth, the water will vanish and that which stays will become thick, fetid, and red like the blood of the deceased person. The stench of the sewage and rotten eggs will be omnipresent. The flora will be slowly dying, leaving the Earth brown and dusty. There will be no wind and no rain. The skin on people's faces will be blistered and bloody, cracked just like the dried ground. These cracks in the ground will be so deep, that all of the underground crud and creatures will resurface. With them, once again, all of the forgotten diseases will attack all of those who will still be alive.

Aliens

20.06.1992

Slawik: And I am blessed again with another vision. The lady's voice whispered into my ear: 'wake up-it is time'. And I saw something comparable to the science-fiction movie. I saw that UFOs, aliens, and all other space creatures, are nothing else but demons. These evil spirits guard their airspace in order to protect, and carry out their missions. The time will come when more people will die in planes and helicopter crashes than in the war. This will be caused not by the faulty equipment, but by the fact that people will violate the demons' airspace. And this will continue to happen until people understand that by intruding demons in space, they also interrupt the preparation for their final war with God. These demons are in contact with the most influential people from our world, with whom they constantly cooperate.

The aliens (demons) often kidnap people, and use them as slaves. I see many places hidden from humanity where missing people work for the demons. The biggest place on Earth where these kidnapped people are enslaved is the well-known Mariana Trench. On its bottom lies a slimy and thick layer of sludge, and other faeces—like sediments. Under these layers is a second bottom, into which the Atlántida slumped centuries ago. This city is well preserved, and strictly secured by the 'UFOs'. All of the kidnapped victims are alive and unaware of who is responsible for what's happened to them. The demons cannot reveal themselves due to their nightmarish appearance, which would make people insane. If the Atlántida was ever inspected, the whole perception about the universe, and UFOs, would completely change. The people would finally understand who their real enemy is, and would simply fight with the beast. The demons cannot allow it. They are afraid of Jesus Christ and therefore are, in a way, limited in what they do. If this wasn't the case, humanity would be long gone. What is important for the demons is the fact that people will die as sinners, after living their life as if God didn't exist, as if there was no such thing as hell. The demons are also often successful in possessing people, who then become their slaves— their living marionettes.

There is one more place which could be discovered by people, which would open up their eyes to evil. This demonic structure is hidden in the mountains, and is also securely guarded by the same evil forces. This construction is similar to a human mind, or a computer, but is much more developed. The demons concealed it from the human eye and camouflaged it as one of the rocks.

Some of the UFOs use diamonds as their spacecraft fuel. The most influential people in the world called The Illuminati, from the world government, provide them with these precious stones. The biggest diamonds always mean the best achievement. And this is why the most famous stone robberies are always linked with many deaths. This, on the other hand could be prevented if these diamonds were stored by the right people.

In the near future, people will learn how to build the same space crafts, but will develop them in a way to allow them to use a different fuel. They will believe that Jesus Christ is our Saviour the only redeemer, and in every flying object will place an unfading lamp, and the icon of the Christ. This will be a very short period, when God will allow humans to battle evil under Heaven's surveillance.

01.07.1992

Walentyna: Slawik often scream when asleep. I rush to his bedroom check if he is OK, but he never is. He lay flat on his back, with eyes half open, and roll back. His hands dangle lifelessly from his bed. I see he not can move but I not allow hold his hands, or speak to him. I only allow stand there and watch. He speak to me that when he get visions I must not disturb him. He must see it all so I stand and watch.

02.07.1992

Slawik: The lady's voice woke me up again. I am not sure how much more I can handle. My body feels weaker, and weaker. Even my mother looks worried, but I do not complain to her at all. I asked the lady how many more visions will I experience, and she answered 'until you die'. I rested my heavy head on the pillow, and waited for the scaring images to attack me one after the other. I see demons every night. They are so close. Some are bony, sticky from the grease cowering them, and some have half a face or no face at all. I can see that no one will be able to understand and imagine their look until the demons reveal themselves to humans. There will be a time when these 'space people' will land their crafts on the Earth pretending to be repressed by evil forces. Humanity will welcome them, and in exchange they will offer analysis of their bodies, and healings if necessary. When the aliens will take a small part of someone's skin for analysis, they will grow a human size skin out of it to be able to pull it on themselves. This way they will be able to pursue their plans in disguise as human beings. These demons will kidnap people they stole the skin from, and will live as they did, in their homes, with their families. The kidnapped ones will be killed, or taken as slaves.

03.07.1992

Walentyna: Slawik speak there will be one scientist who already believes in everything Slawik speak and, together with his colleagues, will construct device similar to binoculars, which will help recognise these demons. Slawik speak: 'Mother, there will be one scientist who, together with his work colleagues, will construct a very smart device intended to uncloak the demons. To check this device, these scientists will meet up in an arranged place. It will be a chilly and very dark night, with no stars, and no moon in the sky. They will hide in an unlit side alley, behind some rusty skips. Soundlessly, after a few hours of waiting, these human-nonhumans will appear. The scientists' heartbeat will increase immediately. What they see in this device is nothing they had expected. They are about to scream and run, but they don't. Somehow, they will find the strength to stay quiet. And this will save their lives.' Slawik speak that they will follow these demons, and observe them closely. And everything they see will be reveal to world. Whole humanity will be warn about kidnappings, and process of skin changing. These devices will be then produce worldwide. Whatever Slawik see, and experience, make all his prophecies almost come alive. It is not case of him see things, but him be there, as if his soul separate from his body, and shift into future.

The Christianity-Baiting

09.01.1993

Walentyna: People speak to me about this satanic system. They want know when it begin. I speak that we all stand on verge of these happenings. I remember Slawik speak to me: 'Mother, you will live to the Antichrist coming.'

09.01.1993

Slawik: The lady left me earlier tonight, but before she was gone she said that this whole Christianity repression will cause massive divisions of the priesthood. Some of the priests will beg people not to take the sign of the beast, and the rest will try to persuade the congregation that it is permissible to be marked. I never asked her anything. The sound of her voice, firm, almost desperate, was saying one thing- the pain. No questions were needed.

It is 01:45am and my mind aches. The lady came again. I feel sad, and defeated. I know one thing though. After my death, I will help all these believers, who did not move to safe places on time. When the time will come, and the homes in Moscow will start to cave in, I will appear on the Earth again to save all these Christians trapped inside them. Also, Holy Mary will appear in various places to warn the Christians of oncoming danger. Together with the angels, we will help these people to evacuate from the decaying cities. This is why it doesn't matter where you are, and in what conditions you live in. You should trust God because He will save His people.

It is 4:15 am and I am still awake. I do not understand why people are so stubborn. You all have to open your eyes. Now! Don't you see anything? Nowadays, in churches, many books are sold about how the Antichrist's servants will offer to people the choice between the bread and the cross. Don't you see, that those who will not hide, will not have any choice to make? I can assure you that these people will be hounded, and marked by force. I saw how every road will have police patrols, therefore the Christians will have to live in the secret settlements, and God will protect them there. I also saw how the rest of humanity will take the mark, and how those who take it will be rewarded with everything they can only imagine. No laws, no poverty, no struggles. They will party, drink, and take drugs. The people in the settlements will be forced to guard their children day and night as the loose life outside these settlements will affect them like hypnosis. Open your eyes, and do it now. You must understand that those who will not betray God will not die. They will not starve and will live to see Christ.

10.01.1993

Walentyna: Slawik cry when speak about Christianity situation. He speak: 'Mother, the change of the Creed will slaughter people's minds. It will have such a huge impact on everyone, that the churches will become empty.' He speak that repress Christians will live in small settlements, and that their situation will be very difficult at beginning, however soon after it will improve as God will hide them from those in power. He speak that: 'The Christians will be invisible to the zombie-police officers. The zombies will not see their homes, the places their live in, and not even themselves.' These zombies, Slawik speak, when standing in front of Christian houses, will only see deserted field and nothing else, and this is how God will hide those who not betray him.

The Execution

15.02.1993

Slawik: It is 12:30am and I just woke up as I was very thirsty. There was nothing to drink in my bedroom so I stood up and went to the kitchen. I could hear my mother's loud snoring. I grabbed some water and went straight back. I closed my bedroom door and noticed a small, white cloud next to my bed. It looked like it was made out of many smaller clouds creating a white rose. And again I heard her voice whispering that the people need to understand that if God will not help, no one will survive.

16.02.1993

Walentyna: Slawik speak to me that deep underground are secret laboratories, where scientists create new species. These beings will be release as soon as scientists abandon their place of work.

17.02.1993

Slawik: After listening to what the lady had to tell me I saw the Earth - how it will be invaded by the vermin. They will crawl out of the toilets, out of the air holes, and all of the places connected in any way with the outside world. The rats and the locusts will also attack. I saw how the rats will repeatedly go out of the cracks in the ground. They will eat people alive, and will walk back into the ground as if someone had steered them. The locusts will fly around in the enormous cloud—like pods, and will kill everything in their way that's still breathing. Even dogs will hide day and night inside their kennels, while shaking in agony and howling. The plague of flies will come almost at the same time as the rest of the creatures. These insects will be as hungry and aggressive as the others, scavenging, and engorging the flesh of dead and alive. The birds, especially the crows, will also attack. Unlike the locusts, the crows will appear unexpectedly, and viciously.

These rabid fowl will rend the human skin. The people will jump from the roofs, they will cut their veins, hang, and drown themselves. The stench in the air, and the crud coming out from the ground from the smashed shrines, will make everyone sick, even the animals. Everyone will be covered in abscesses, and blotches. Everyone except those who didn't betray God.

Then I saw how those who take the sign of the beast will be sick. They will be so weak that often they will crawl, and grovel. The animals also will be infected. Most of them will have rabies. Their skin will be paper-thin, and broken in places. It will rot and reek, leaving them cowered in pus, and blood. The animals' eyes will be opaque, and they will be befuddled. They will not fear anybody, and this will make them more dangerous. All these infected animals will shift in massive flocks from the woods straight onto people.

18.02.1993

Walentyna: Slawik often compare the Earth with death camp where human remains was everywhere. Slawik speak 'mother, in the near future, the Earth will change into a massive grave, where there won't be even a patch of ground devoid of human blood.'

23.02.1993

Walentyna: I still remember one day Slawik is late from school, and I get really anxious. As soon as he back, I want to shout, but I freeze. He come with this huge smile on his face, and his eyes wide open. He look like he is inject with massive dose of enthusiasm and energy. His hands is cross tightly on his chest, under which I see something. Slawik hold big box. He rush to kitchen table, where he place it on. He grab box handle and, really slowly, begin to open it. My heart rush like crazy. When he finally open it, my heart stop. My little boy buy me box full of tools. Few days later he also bring home military shovel. He not understand why so many people wouldn't listen to him, but he speak that 'at least you mother will be prepared.'

24.02.1993

Slawik: My body slowly releases the rest energy it has left. Sasha doesn't come to my room anymore. I heard him saying to my mother that he is scared to look at me. But he needs to. I asked him to come. He had fear in his eyes. He froze in the doorway, rubbed his fists against each other, battling with himself. I said: 'come, please'. He walked in and sat on the bed next to me.

'What is it that you need?' He asked quietly.

'I need you to write my words, everything that I say you need to write down.' I said.

'Why don't you ask your mother?' Sasha asked.

'She knows it all and I want you to finally understand the reason I was sent here.' I replied. Sasha left my room saying nothing, but returned shortly after with a smile on his face saying: 'I will do this for you brother.'

Then the fifth angel poured out his bowl on the throne of the beast, and his kingdom became darkened; and they gnawed their tongues because of pain, and they blasphemed the God of heaven because of their pains and their sores; and they did not repent of their deeds

(Revelation 16:11).

03.03.1993

Later this evening Sasha knocked on my bedroom door. He grabbed the rusty handle and gently pushed it open. I was asleep. He walked in slowly placing his feet one by one on the wooden floorboards. His legs froze just a few steps away from my bed on a squeaky floor panel. I woke up. I tried to open my eyes but my eyelids were stuck together with the draining pus. Sasha went to the kitchen and brought a small wet flannel. My hands felt so heavy I could not lift them up. Sasha placed the flannel on my eyes and wiped them clean. My eyelids raise a bit and I saw Sasha's white teeth next to my face. He looked very happy. He wore his favourite black t-shirt and black trousers that had a few small holes on both knees. Sasha carried a tray with a few biscuits and a glass of water. He placed the tray on the side table, raised my head up with his hand and apposed the glass to my lips. I drank it all with one sip.

'I am dying.' I whispered.

'Yes, you are.' He replied.

His gentle smile, and quiet voice kept me calm, as if he knew that my condition was just something normal and common. He grabbed my favourite notepad and red pencil from the top of my desk, and jumped onto a rocking chair opposite me. With the pen and paper in his hands, Sasha rocked himself on the chair while waiting for me to start. My head was spinning. My thoughts were screaming inside my head 'you have to rush, you have to tell Sasha everything before it will be too late.' I lifted my sweaty body higher on the pillow to improve the air flow into my narrowed trachea. The moving blanket uncovered drops of blood on my pyjama.

Sasha asked, 'How much time do you need to get ready?'

'I am sorry.' I said. I forgot how impatient he was. He always liked to sort everything out as soon as possible, and I was only slowing him down.

'I am sorry Sasha, You can start writing.' I added.

***To All Humanity- 3 Days of Darkness* by Slawik Kraszennikow (written one day before his death)**

'And I heard her warm, soothing voice again. It was about two o'clock in the morning. I was tired. This time the vision was different. I was watching it all knowing there will not be any more to be seen. The three days of darkness was the last of my visions given to me by our Lord.

'Now, the time of reckoning is coming. This is the end of the world that humanity created and the beast ruled. You will know when the time has come. You must secure all the doors, cover all the windows, and seal every hole in your home. Do not open them. When the time will come do not look through the windows. Light the blessed candles. You have to have enough of them to last you for many days and nights. Pray with the Holy Rosary, and do it with your hands raised up to heaven, or prostrate yourselves. Do this to save many souls. When the time will come, you will be forbidden to go outside, so store as much food as possible. The power of nature will be shaken, and the fire storm will fill the humanity with terror. Be brave. I am, and will be among you all.'

'Ha ha.' Sasha gasped out while laughing. 'You and your drama. Your brain is steamed from the high fever. There were no visions, no voices only you're deprived from the oxygen brain.'

'Sasha, please, don't. It will not take much longer. Please just write.'

'Ok, whatever, the crazy talk to be continued.' Sasha sighed.

'Make sure all your animals will be safe during these days. Seal their kennels, and provide them with food and water. Do this before God's anger will strike. You will be given the signs before these happenings to allow you the time to prepare yourselves, and your animals. You will be forbidden to leave your house during these days, as God doesn't want you to see his anger. Those who will not obey the Lord's will, will die. Make sure every window in your house is cowered completely. God told me: "I am the Lord of the whole of creation, and the people's faith obligates me to rush to help those who shall not betray me. The hour of My coming is close! However, I shall show mercy."'

Sasha stood up, walked to the window and said: 'So your great God will kill the humanity, and will show how kind he is by saving a few? This is you convincing me to trust and be faithful to Him? I think the antichrist is a better option for anyone who wants to be saved, don't you think?'

'No, never.' I raised my voice. 'The Earth needs to be reborn and that's that.' My heart was rushing so fast I could not catch a breath. Sasha turned around and rushed to kitchen for more water.

'I am sorry.' He said. 'Please drink and calm down. I will write anything you want me to, just please calm down. We don't want your mother to disturb us do we?' He added.

'You are right, we don't, let's continue with these notes.' I gasped.

'I can see a few of His angels on guard. They are enormous, blinding white creatures, who will be the executors of His will. I can see them standing one next to the other. They hold, gold, and sharp swords, a few meters long. They will be the obliterators of those who derided His name, and didn't believe in His divine revelation. But the

Lord will show mercy to those who didn't get the sign of the beast. They will know when to hide, and when to pray. And they will suffer no harm. Everything that has been foreseen must happen so that God will prove for the last time that He is the only divine Creator of all. God will not disown those who spread His word, and will not disown those who beg the Virgin Mary for help.

'I saw the night of when everything will happen. That night will be freezing cold, and the wind will give almost pained— like sounds. It will howl and moan as if it was alive. Soon after, lightning bolts will strike the Earth, and the ground will begin to shake. Close your doors immediately, and cover all windows. Do not let anybody in from the outside. Kneel down in front of the cross, repent, and beg the Holy Mary for her protection. During the earthquakes, do not look through windows as the God's rage is Holy. I can see those who didn't obey His will, they are lying on the floor, dead.

'The hurricane winds will bring toxic gases from around the Atlantic Ocean, and will spread them across the whole world. Every innocent who dies during these three days, will become a martyr, and will go straight to heaven. I saw others, the individuals with the gift of visions. I saw them in Belgium, Switzerland, and Spain.'

'And China.' Sasha sounded like a guinea pig's squeal.

'If you say so,' I whispered.

'They were chosen to help prepare their own countries for what's coming.' I continued. 'I saw the year 1950. It was the beginning. The war that began in 1950 was the starter for all these near happenings. The world is drunk with sin. All humanity is fearless. The people must be punished. The atheists, the strippers, those who are ashamed to go to church, their judgment day is near. This day will strike as quick as a flash of light, when the needed sunrise will not appear. From this moment you cannot leave your homes. You have to completely trust in His mercy, especially those of you who suffer from anxiety, and heart problems. Many people will not listen. The pandemonium caused by the gloom will poison the world, and thousands of people will die from despair, and petrification.'

'Do you understand now why people need to know what will happen to them? Do you see why everyone including you must be prepared?' I asked.

'Yes, yes, they need to know to have a chance to save themselves. That's why these notes, that's why you are here, that's why I am here. Please, oh please tell me more.' Sasha said while looking at my clock and shaking his legs.

'What's wrong?' I asked.

He turned away and said: 'I wasted your time on talking nonsense, I just want you to finish it. I am sorry.' He finally understood, I thought.

'Ok, we need to finish it now,' I added.

'I saw a comet very close to the Earth, encircling the planet for about two weeks. And I saw others staring at the sky with hope that it will not strike. Then I saw how the comet gets closer, and closer, and finally hits the bottom of the Atlantic Ocean. I was even able to see the exact moment of when the fire ball eats into the Earth's crust. It almost breaks the globe in half, creating an underwater crater the size of Africa. Then I saw how the Earth was thrown off its orbit for three days. The volcanos activity will be very high before the comet strikes, however the collision with Earth will cause the deformation of the Earth's crust, and the most aggressive eruptions ever that will release black smoke that will cover the sun. I also saw thousands of other volcanos awakened due to this crash, and erupting poisonous lava, and gases. The merge of discharging chemicals will cause a complete blackout. The magnetic poles will be swapped around, and for a short time only, the planet's orbit will be changed for a bigger one. The sun's gravity will rectify the Earth's orbit, however before this happens the temperature on the planet will drastically drop. During these three days, the caves, and the underground will best protect against the cold, and the sulphur, that at that time will consume the oxygen whilst spreading across the Earth. The air will be deprived of oxygen. It will be almost impossible to breathe. The underground will not be as badly affected.'

'I need water, please give me some water,' I asked Sasha. My voice got weaker, and quieter. I felt fresh blood on my dry teeth. My lips cracked in many places. Sasha gave me water and after a few seconds put the glass back on the side table. Drops of blood were inside it. 'Not much longer.' I said. Sasha grabbed his notes and sat back down on the chair ready to continue.

'Please write,' I said.

'I also saw how the fire storms burn alive those who will revolt, and stay outside. I heard moans, and the children's lament, and saw how it pushes many to suicide. The air will be so heavy, it will appear as a grey fog floating high above the ground, and consuming place by place. This will change the streets and alleys into ubiquitous eco—like passageways through which the noise of dying people will fly. Then I looked at the sky again. The stars were moving quickly, almost as aggressively as the comet that hit the globe. I couldn't see the

Plough, and the Little Dipper anymore. The sky was red, and black. It changed.

'Every impious being will be obliterated to allow the righteous to rule the new world. The purification of the world will take a day and a night, and will continue throughout the next day and night, and another day. The amount of deaths will be greater than in the two world wars combined. Three quarters of humanity will be wiped out. During that time hell will release its demons. They will think the beast rules the world. It will, but only for three days. Hell will help to cleanse the Earth of everything that's villainous. On the third night all these demons will be exiled back to hell, and the stars will shine once again. The next day the sun will brightly illuminate the whole sky, and those who survived will be able to leave their homes. It will be the time of revival and rebirth. The new renaissance.'

Then I saw Him who told me: 'the damages on Earth will be great! However, I, your Lord, will rebuild the world. I am with you.'

(1 Samuel 15:1-35)

Sasha closed the notes, stood up with an even bigger smile and said: 'You are so stupid, I cannot even believe how fucked up your brain is. What do you think I will do with these notes? Do you think I will copy them and send them all across the world, to China maybe?'

Is my head playing tricks on me? Was I hearing Sasha right? No, it is impossible.

I asked: 'What did you say?' Sasha came closer, turned around and uncovered the skin from under his hair at the back of his head. I saw three numbers 666 scarred on his skin. *'What…'* I could not finish my question. My head dropped, paralysed on the pillow. I felt my chest moving rapidly up and down. I could not catch up with my breathing. The shallow puffs of air escaped from my mouth, and even less I managed to inhale back into my lungs.

Sasha looked at me and said: 'What-what? What is this? You stupid, weak being. This is what you are - weak, and almost dead, ha-ha.'

'But you are Sasha, my little brother. Why did you mark yourself? Is this another of your silly jokes?' I asked.

'You are an idiot. I am the antichrist, I am the one who makes your body sick, and I was the one who killed Wiktoria.

All the memories, from when I tried to help Wiktoria, came back to me. The images of her ginger hair, pale, bony face and bruised body, were now flashing in front of my eyes. I analysed again everything that has happened. I scanned her, I healed her. I also asked Sasha to hold her back when she was unsteady. I saw him staring at her constantly. But he was just observing, was he? My thoughts were crushing me from the inside. He was just observing, and he run away upset when she passed out.

'You were so upset when she died, you run away crying, I don't understand.' I said.

'I was laughing not crying, ha-ha. I had to leave. Seeing her on the ground, and seeing your pale face when she collapsed was hilarious. I cried laughing you idiot. Do you think that only you can scan somebody? I do that too. Easy. It wasn't really that hard to crush her insides again. It also isn't hard to make you sick.'

'But why?' I asked. My eyes welled up. 'You are my brother.' I said

'Do you think Maria will ever believe you again, or her relatives and friends?' Sasha said. 'No, no one will. Your stupidity makes me laugh, day and night. And your backward mother - she felt there was something wrong, but you didn't listen and you know why?

Because you decided to trust your abandoned brother more than your own backward mother.'

'But, but, what? No. What?' I gasped. I could feel my throat closing down. I could not swallow.

'Next time you will know better - but there will not be next time because you will be dead soon. Your body is eaten up from the inside by me, ha-ha. Stupid, stupid, stupid. And you know what else? I wasn't abandoned. I made them drown themselves.'

Sasha's parents didn't go out too often. Their faces were dead, no emotions, black circles around their eyes. The windows, doors everything covered. My mother used to say these people were very private. Was he really the reason they were so private? No. No. Wait. What?

'They were as weak as you are. I heard them talking about you, they wanted to save me - me! - the antichrist.'

'The voice I heard told me not to trust anyone. You tried to convince me that it was my mother brainwashing me. She didn't trust you.' I said. I placed one fist on my chest and hit myself as hard as I could. 'I trusted him, the beast, and I am the chosen one?' I thought.

'Your mother didn't trust me then, but she trusts me now.' Sasha replied.

These words like blades cut up my heart. I must stand up. I have to stop him. I grabbed the side panels of my bed and pulled myself up a bit, but dropped back down like a stone. My chest was moving faster and faster, I couldn't breathe. I started to gasp for air, I was choking.

The front door opened. My mother came back home.

'Shit. I wear my best mourning clothes today and that bitch came back earlier.' Sasha said. He grabbed my notes, and diary and ran away. I wanted to do something but my body didn't let me. I couldn't shout, not even speak. The images of the antichrist were flashing in front of me. He was living with us the whole time, he kissed my mother, and cuddled me. Every day my health deteriorated and he was the reason. 'Why nobody told me?' I screamed inside my head. The blood started to flow from my mouth. By the time my mother came to check on me my fever was so high that sweat and blood were dripping down my face. As she walked into the room, the room span and I lost consciousness.

17.03.1993

Walentyna: I carry Slawik to hospital on my hands. Doctors take him straight to ICU. After few hour they speak that they is unable to diagnose him. They speak that it look like something suck up most of blood from his tiny body. They speak that his organs is take over by something, so aggressive that it is impossible to even recognise when, and how, it start. Doctor tell me I can go see him. I rush to him straight away. I see Slawik on bed, pale, connect to white machine. He wake up and fall back to sleep. Next day morning he wake up, I am still next to him. He wave his finger to me so I come closer. He whisper: 'Mummy… I… Sasha… I want you to know…'

'I am here, darling, tell me, I listen son.' I speak but he fell asleep again. I move closer to his ear and speak 'I will take care of Sasha. I know how much you love him'. I cannot stop crying. He is so weak but strong.

-1:45am

Walentyna: Slawik regain conscious but fell back to sleep. He moan while unconscious, 'Sasha, antichrist, don't trust.'

I stop him and speak 'You want Sasha help me warn people and save them. I know son, don't worry. Sasha will help.' I place my fingers on his mouth to stop him speak and stop his breathing getting unsteady again. I speak over and over again that Sasha is safe. I not able speak anything else to him to make him feel better so I rest my head next to his shoulder and I sing him his favourite song:

Ах, мама, маменька,	*My mother, my mummy*
Я уж не маленький!	*I am not little anymore!*
Ах, мама, маменька	*My mother, my mummy*
Мне много лет...	*I am really old...*

Slawik touched my hand and with close eyes whisper:

'Mummy, your voice sounds exactly like the one I was hearing.'

I kiss his forehead and speak: 'I know son.'

-4:45am

Doctor call me. When I leave his room I see Sasha in corridor. He wear his black clothes again, same clothes he had on when his parents left him. He look so worry. I tell him to go see Slawik because he is very sick. Sasha cuddle me and go. I speak with doctor and hear alarm coming from Slawik room. His heart stop. Doctor try do something but Sasha don't let Slawik hand go. He push doctor away and try save my baby. He check if Slawik still breathe. Place head on Slawik chest to listen for heartbeat, but there is none. I manage to pull Sasha on side to let doctor help, but it is too late. I look at Sasha and want to hold him in arms but poor thing run away. He must be devastate.

-4:50am

Walentyna: Slawik passed away 17th March 1993 at 4:50 in morning. I come back home at 10am and sit on his empty bed. I look at his clock and see it stop at time he die. It did not restart since. I notice Slawik desk is empty, his diary gone, and all notes disappear. Sasha not return yet but leave note for me: 'I will be back.' My eyes is red, I cannot stop tears. This boy, who I not trust on beginning, go and do what Slawik ask him to do. He take my son notes to warn every one of antichrist. I can rest assure now that Sasha redeem Slawik wishes. And when he come back Slawik bedroom will be his. My Sasha.

And he said to me:

'These words are trustworthy and true.

And the Lord, the God of the spirits of the prophets,

has sent his angel to show his servants

what must soon take place.'

(Revelation 22:6)

Slawik's notes found under his bed after his death:

The Twin Tower Crash- 2001

The False Pope Francis- 2013

The Ebola Outbreak- 2014

The Microchips- Italy- 2015

The Syrian Conflict- 2014-2016

The World War 3- 2021

The Comet Strikes-

www.ingramcontent.com/pod-product-compliance
Lightning Source LLC
LaVergne TN
LVHW010455160826
845677LV00012B/2491
9798652902186